P9-DZA-645

EARTHBORN

PROLOGUE

Once, long ago, the computer of the starship *Basilica* had governed the planet Harmony for forty million years. Now it watched over a much smaller population, and with far fewer powers to intervene. But the planet that it tended to was Earth, the ancient home of the human race.

It was the starship *Basilica* that brought a group of humans home again, only to find that in the absence of humanity, two new species had reached the lofty pinnacle of intelligence. Now the three peoples shared a vast massif of high mountains, lush valleys, and a climate that varied more with elevation than with latitude.

The diggers called themselves the earth people, making tunnels through the soil and into the trunks of trees they hollowed out. The angels were the sky people, building roofed nests in trees and hanging upside down from limbs to sleep, to argue, and to teach. The humans were the middle people now, living in houses above the ground.

There was no digger city without human houses on the ground above it, no angel village without the walled chambers of the middle people providing artificial caves. The vast knowledge that the humans brought with them from the planet Harmony was only a fraction of what their ancestors had known on Earth before their exile forty million years before. Now even that was mostly lost; yet what remained was so far superior to what the people of the earth and sky had known that wherever the middle people dwelt, they had great power, and usually ruled.

In the sky, however, the computer of the starship *Basilica* forgot nothing, and through satellites it had deployed around the Earth it watched, it collected data and remembered everything it learned.

Nor was it alone in its watching. For inside it lived a woman who had come to Earth with the first colonists; but then, clothed in the cloak of the starmaster, she returned into the sky, to sleep long years and waken briefly, her body healed and helped by the cloak, so that death, if it could ever come to her at all, was still a far distant visitor. She remembered everything that mattered to her, remembered people who had once lived and now were gone. Birth and life and death, she had seen so much of it that she barely noticed it now. It was all generations to her, seasons in her garden, trees and grass and people rising and falling, rising and falling.

On Earth there was a little bit of memory as well. Two books, written on thin sheets of metal, had been maintained since the return of the humans. One was in the hands of the king of the Nafari, passed down from king to king. The other, less copious, had been passed to the brother of the first king, and from him to his sons, who were not kings, not even famous men, until at last, unable now even to read the ancient script, the last of that line gave the smaller metal book into the hands of the man who was king in his day. Only in the pages of those books was there a memory that lasted, unchanged, from year to year.

At the heart of the books, in the depths of the ship's records, and warm in the soul of the woman, the greatest of the memories was this: that the human beings had been brought back to Earth, called by an entity they did not understand, the one who was called the Keeper of Earth. The Keeper's voice was not clear, nor was the Keeper understandable as the ship's computer was, back in the days when it was called the Oversoul and people worshipped it as a god. Instead the Keeper spoke through dreams, and, while many received the dreams, and many believed that they had meaning, only a few knew who it was that sent them, or what it was the Keeper wanted from the people of Earth.

You planned your plans, you plotted your plots, and you never asked humans for advice. Instead you roped us in and dragged us to Earth transformed our lives forever and now you ask *me* if any of this makes sense? What happened to the master plan?"

"My plan was simple," said the Oversoul. "Get back to Earth and ask the Keeper what I should do about the weakening power of the Oversoul of Harmony. I fulfilled that plan as far as I could. Here I am."

"And here *I* am."

"Don't you see, Shedemei? Your being here wasn't *my* plan. I needed human help to assemble one workable starship, but I didn't need to take any humans with me. I brought you because the Keeper of Earth was somehow sending you dreams—and sending them faster than light, I might add. The Keeper seemed to want you humans here. So I brought you. And I came, expecting to find technological marvels waiting for me. Machines that could repair me, replenish me, send me back to Harmony able to restore the power of the Oversoul. Instead I wait here, I've waited nearly five hundred years—"

"As have I," added Shedemei.

"You've slept through most of them," said the Oversoul. "And you don't have responsibility for a planet a hundred lightyears distant where technology is beginning to blossom and devastating wars are only a few generations away. I don't have time for this. Except that if the Keeper thinks I have time for it, I probably do. Why doesn't the Keeper talk to me? When no one was hearing anything for all these years, I could be patient. But now humans are dreaming again, the Keeper is on the move again, and yet still it says nothing to me."

"And you ask *me?*" said Shedemei. "You're the one who should have memories dating back to the time when you were created. The Keeper sent you, right? Where was it then? *What* was it then?"

"I don't know." If a computer could shrug, Shedemei imagined the Oversoul would do it now. "Do you think I haven't searched my memory? Before your husband died, he helped me search, and we found nothing. I remember the Keeper always being present, I remember knowing that certain vital instructions had been programmed into me by the Keeper—but as to who or what the Keeper is or was or even might have been, I know as little as you."

"Fascinating," said Shedemei. "Let's see if we can think of a way to get the Keeper to talk to you. Or at least to show her hand."

Mon was seated, as usual, down at the stewards' end of the table. His father told him that the king's second son was placed there in order to show respect for the record-keepers and message-bearers and treasurers and provisioners, for, as Father said, "If it weren't for them, there'd be no kingdom for the soldiers to protect."

When Father said that, Mon had answered, in his most neutral voice, "But if you really want to show your respect for them, you'd place Ha-Aron among them."

To which Father mildly replied, "If it weren't for the army, all the stewards would be dead."

So Mon, the second son, was all that the second rank of leaders in the kingdom merited; the first son was the honor of the first rank, the military men, the people who really mattered.

And that was how the business of dinner was conducted, too. The King's Supper had begun many generations ago as a council of war— that was when women began to be excluded. In those days it was only once a week that the council ate together, but for generations now it had been every night, and human men of wealth and standing imitated the king in their own homes, dining separately from their wives and daughters. It wasn't that way among the sky people, though. Even those who shared the king's table went home and sat with their wives and children for another meal.

Which was why, sitting at Mon's left hand, the chief clerk, the old angel named bGo, was barely picking at his food. It was well known that bGo's wife became quite miffed if he showed no appetite at *her* table, and Father had always refused to be offended that bGo apparently feared his wife more than he feared the king. bGo was senior among the clerks, though as head of the census he was certainly not as powerful as the treasuremaster and the provisioner. He was also a surly conversationalist and Mon hated having to sit with him.

Beyond bGo, though, his otherself, Bego, was far more talkative— and had a much sturdier appetite, mostly because he had never married. Bego, the recordkeeper, was only a minute and a half less senior than bGo, but one would hardly imagine they were the same age, Bego had so much energy, so much vigor, so much . . . so much anger, Mon thought sometimes. Mon loved school whenever Bego was their tutor, but he sometimes wondered if Father really knew how much rage seethed under the surface of his recordkeeper. Not disloyalty—Mon would report *that* at once. Just a sort of general anger at life. Aronha said it was because he had never once mated with a female in his life, but then Aronha had sex on the brain these days and thought that lust explained everything—which, in the case of Aronha and all his friends, was no doubt true. Mon didn't know why Bego was so angry. He just knew that it put a delicious skeptical edge on all of Bego's lessons. And even on his eating. A sort of savagery in the way he lifted the panbread rolled up with bean paste to his lips and bit down on it. The way he ground the food in his jaws when he chewed, slowly, methodically, glaring out at the rest of the court.

On Mon's right, the treasuremaster and the provisioner were caught up in their own business conversation—quietly, of course, so as not to distract from the *real* meeting going on at the king's end of the table, where the soldiers were regaling each other with anecdotes from recent raids and skirmishes. Being adult humans, the treasuremaster and provisioner were much taller than Mon and generally ignored him after the initial courtesies. Mon was more the height of the sky people to his left, and besides, he knew Bego better, and so when he talked at all, it was to them.

"I have something I want to tell Father," said Mon to Bego.

Bego chewed twice more and swallowed, fixing Mon with his weary gaze all the while. "Then tell him," he said.

"Exactly," murmured bGo.

"It's a dream," said Mon.

"Then tell your mother," said Bego. "Middle women still pay attention to such things."

"Right," murmured bGo.

"But it's a true dream," said Mon.

bGo sat up straight. "And how would you know that."

Mon shrugged. "I know it."

bGo turned to Bego, who turned to him. They gazed at each other, as if some silent communication were passing between them. Then Bego turned back to Mon. "Be careful about making claims like that."

"I am," said Mon. "Only when I'm sure. Only when it matters."

That was something Bego had taught them in school, about making they knew that if the men there, diggers or humans, knew of the Nafari walking along this narrow shelf of land, there would be such an outcry, and soon war parties would be scaling the cliff walls. Not that this spelled sure death, outnumbered though they might be. Even diggers, born to climb, would have a hard time getting up the rocks. But eventually the Elemaki would either reach their shelf and force them to fight to the last man, or the Nafari would have to climb higher and higher until they reached the altitudes where men freeze or faint or grow mad.

So they continued to move silently and smoothly along the rock, wearing their earth-colored tunics and leggings, their earth-colored blankets draped and pinned over their shoulders, their very skin and hair smeared with dirt to make them blend better into the stony cliff.

If only we could find a way to go up and over these mountains and avoid this heavily-populated lake, thought Monush. And then a thought burst into his mind. Of course we can! Just back there behind us there's a. . . . there's a. . . . He couldn't remember. What was it he was thinking of? Something behind them? Why? There were no pursuers. Had he forgotten one of his men? He stopped and made a quick count. All were there—and, because they had stopped, most were gaping down at the holy lake below them. Monush beckoned them on. The shelf rose again. They passed by the long lake, sleeping only two nights with it in view.

After the lake, they passed through easier country, though it was all the more dangerous. It was a large region of lowish mountains, green to their tops, and every valley had at least some people in it, usually diggers, often humans as well, and now and then an isolated settlement of angels, though most of these were either slaves to a nearby Elemaki village or were "free"—but still tributary to one Elemaki king or another. Several times they were spotted by angels soaring overhead, but instead of crying out a warning, the angels always flew on, ignoring them. One angel even swooped low and landed on a nearby branch, then pointed down the ridge that Monush and his men were following and shook his head. Don't go this way, he was saying. Monush nodded, bowed to him as to a friend, and the angel rose up into the air and flew away.

It's good for *us*, at least, thought Monush, that the Elemaki are so harsh on the few angels forced to live among them. It gives us friends wherever we go. Weak friends, it's true, but friends are all welcome in the land of our enemies.

On the fortieth day of their expedition, they came to a place where four streams met within a few rods. The water was turbulent, and yet no diggers or humans or angels lived near it. "A holy place like this," whispered Chem, "and yet no one dwells here to receive the gift?"

Monush nodded, then smiled. "Perhaps they receive the gift downstream."

He led them on, just a little way, and as they moved downstream they saw that no new hills seemed to rise up ahead of them. The land was about to change.

And suddenly they understood. For the ground dropped away in front of them. The water of the river soared out like an arrow's flight, spouting into the air and then falling as perpetual rain down onto the valley below. It was a place of power, the only place that Monush had ever seen or heard of where water from a stream turned directly into rain without first rising up into the sky as clouds.

"Is there a way down?" asked Chem.

"As you said," answered Monush. "It's a holy place. See? Many feet have come up this cliff."

It was almost a stairway, the descent was so artificial, steps cut into the stone, earth held in place by planks. "A cripple could climb here," said Alekiam, the one who spoke the dialect of digger language that was most common among the Elemaki. Not that they were likely to run across many diggers who hadn't adopted Torg, the trading language that was mostly the original human language, with pronunciations adapted to the mouths of diggers and angels and thousands of their words thrown in. But it was possible, here in these high mountains, where it was said that in some remote valleys diggers and angels still lived together in the old way, the diggers stealing statues made by the angels and bringing them home to worship them as gods— even as they sent raiding parties to kidnap the children of the angels and eat them. No one in living memory had run across such a place, but few doubted that people like that might yet survive—diggers who called the angels "skymeat," and angels who called the diggers "devils," both with good reason.

"Quiet," said Monush. "This place is well traveled. Who knows who might be at the bottom?"

But there was no one at the bottom, and the land, being lower, had different fruits in season. Monush led his men to the brow of a hill overlooking the river that flowed away from the perpetual rainstorm at the base of the cliff. He told twelve of them to stay there and keep watch, eating what fruit they could find within sight of each other, while Monush himself took Alekiam, Chem, and a strong soldier named Lemech, who could break a man's neck just by slapping him on the ear.

As they moved carefully along the rivercourse, they could see signs that once this land had been heavily settled. The boundaries of old fields could still be clearly seen, though they were overgrown. And here and there they passed an area that had been cleared and crusted over with stone, so that no diggers could get silently underneath and burrow their way into people's homes.

"Where are all the people?" asked Chem, as they stood in the middle of one such place. "They built well, and now they're gone."

"No they're not," said Lemech.

A tall young human stood at the forest's edge. He had not been there a moment before.

"Hail, friend," said Monush, for he could hardly hope to avoid an encounter now.

At a signal from the tall young man, at least thirty soldiers stepped onto the platform of stone. Where had they been? Hadn't they circled this place before stepping out onto it?

"Lay down your weapons," said Monush softly.

"In a digger's heart I will," said Lemech.

"They have us," said Monush. "If we surrender, perhaps we'll live long enough for the others to find us."

"For all we know these are the people we've come to find," said Chem. "Not a digger among them."

That was true enough. So they laid down their weapons on the stone floor of the platform.

At once the strangers closed on them, seized them, bound them, and forced them to run with them through the woods until they came to a place where twenty such platforms were clustered. On them many buildings rose, most of them houses, but not humble ones, and some of the buildings could not have been houses at all, but rather were palaces and gamecourts, temples and, most prominent of all, one solitary tower rising taller than any of the trees. From that tower you could sure look out over this whole land, thought Monush, and see any enemies that might be approaching.

If the soldiers hadn't gagged Monush and his men, he might have asked them if they were the Zenifi. As it was, they were thrown into a room that must have been built for storing food, but now was empty except for the four bound prisoners.

In Edhadeya's dream, thought Monush, weren't the Zenifi *asking* to be rescued?

Akma awoke from his dream, trembling with fear. But he dared not cry aloud, for they had learned that the diggers who guarded them regarded all loud voices in the night as prayers to the Keeper—and Pabulog had decreed that any praying to the Keeper by these followers of Akmaro was blasphemy, to be punished by death. Not that a single cry in the night would have a child killed—but the diggers would have dragged them out of their tent and beaten them, demanding that they confess that one of them had been praying. The children had learned to waken silently, no matter how terrible the dream.

Still, he had to speak of it while it was fresh in mind. He wanted to waken his mother, wanted her to enfold him in her arms and comfort him. But he was too old for that, he knew; he would be ashamed of needing her comfort even as he gratefully received it.

So it was his father, Akmaro, that he nudged until his father rolled over and whispered, "What is it, Akma?"

"I dreamed."

"A true dream?"

"The Keeper sent men to rescue us. But a cloud of darkness and a mist of water blocked their view and they lost the path to us. Now they will never come."

"How did you know the Keeper sent them?"

"I just knew."

"Very well," said Akmaro. "I will think about this. Go back to sleep."

Akma knew that he had done all he could do. Now it was in his father's hands. He should have been satisfied, but he was not satisfied at all. In fact, he was angry. He didn't want his father to think about it, he wanted his father to *talk* about it. He wanted to help come up with the interpretation of the dream. It *was* his own dream, after all. But his father listened, took the dream seriously enough, but then assumed that it was up to him alone to decide what to do about it, as if Akma were a machine like the Index in the ancient stories.

I'm not a machine, said Akma silently, and I can think of what this means as well as anyone.

It means . . . it means. . . .

That the Keeper sent men to rescue us and they lost the way. What else could it mean? How could Father interpret it any differently?

Maybe it isn't the interpretation of the dream that Father is thinking about. Maybe he's thinking about what to do next. If the Keeper was just going to send another party of rescuers, then why send me such a dream? It must mean that there will be no other rescuers. So it's up to us to save ourselves.

And Akma drifted off to sleep with dreams of battle in his mind, standing sword-in-hand, facing down his tormentors. He saw himself standing over the beheaded body of Pabul; he heard Udad groan with his guts spilled out into his lap as he sat on the ground, marveling at the mess young Akma had made of his body. As for Didul, Akma imagined a long confrontation between them, with Didul finally pleading for his life, the arrogance wiped off his face, his beautiful cheeks streaked with tears. Shall I let you live, after you beat me and taunted me every day for weeks and weeks? For the insult to me, I might forgive you. But shall I let you live, after you slapped my sister so many times until she cried? Shall I let you live, after you drove the other children to exhaustion until the weakest of them collapsed in the hot sun and you laughed as you covered them with mud as if they were dead? Shall I let you live, as you did all these things in front of the parents of these children, knowing that they were helpless to protect their young ones? That was the cruelest thing, to humiliate our parents, to make them weak in front of their own children. And for that, Didul . . . for that, the blade through the neck, your head spinning in the air, bouncing and dancing along the ground before it rolls to rest at the feet of your own father. Let him weep, that cruel tyrant, let him try to push your head back into place and make your vicious little smile come back to your lips, but he can't do it, can he? Pow-

71

erless, isn't he? Standing there with little Muwu clinging to his leg, begging me to spare him at least one son, at least the last of his boys, but I'll spare no one because you spared no one.

With such wistful imaginings did Akma go back to sleep.

Monush was dragged out of his sleep by two men, who seized him by his bound arms and hauled him out of the dank storehouse. He could hear that the others were being treated the same, but he could see nothing because the light of day dazzled his eyes. He was barely able to see clearly when he was hauled before the court of the king.

For that is who it clearly was, though he was the same man who had shown himself before them on the day they were taken. He had not looked like a king then, and even now, Monush thought he was young and seemed unsure of himself. He sat well on the throne, and he commanded with certainty and assurance, but . . . Monush couldn't place what was wrong. Except, perhaps, that this man did not seem to want to be where he was.

What was this strange reluctance? Did he not want to be sitting in judgment on these strangers? Or did he not want to be king?

"Do you understand my language?" asked the king.

"Yes," said Monush. The accent was a little odd, but nothing to be much remarked upon. No one in Darakemba would have mistaken him for one of the Elemaki.

"I am Ak-Ilihi, son of Nuab, who once was Nuak, the king of the Zenifi. My grandfather, Zenifab, led our people out of the land of Darakemba to possess again the land of Nafai, which was the proper inheritance of the Nafari, and he was made king by the voice of the people. It is by that same right that I now rule. Now tell me why you were so bold as to come near the walls of the city of Zidom, while I myself was outside the city with my guards. It was because of your boldness and fearlessness that I decided not to allow my guards to put you to death without first knowing from your own lips how you dared to violate every treaty and defy our rule within the boundaries of that small kingdom that the Elemaki have left to us."

The king waited.

"You are now permitted to speak," the king said.

Monush took a step forward and bowed before Ilihiak. "O King, I am very grateful before the Keeper of Earth that I have been left alive,

"O king," he said, "you have listened to my words many times when we went to war against the Elemaki. Now, O king, if my counsel has ever been of service to you, I beg you to listen to me now and I will be your true servant and deliver this nation out of bondage."

Monush wondered at the formality of Khideo's speech—hadn't he already spoken up several times, just like any of the other men?

Ilihiak touched his hand to his own lips, then opened his palm toward Khideo. "I give my voice to Khideo now."

Ah, so that was it. Khideo wasn't just giving casual counsel. He was asserting a privilege, and Ilihiak had granted it. More was at stake here than just advising the king. If Khideo's plan was accepted, apparently he would be the one to lead the exodus. No doubt Khideo feared that Monush would try to lead the Zenifi out of captivity; Khideo was forestalling any such possibility. Monush would have to be their guide back to Darakemba, and it would be Monush who would introduce them to the great Motiak. But Khideo had no intention of letting Monush supplant him—or Ilihiak—as leader of the nation until the last possible moment. How needless this maneuvering was; Monush was not a man who cared who was in command, as long as the plan they followed was a wise one.

"The great Motiak sent so few men to find us because any larger group would surely have been caught and destroyed by the Elemaki," said Khideo.

Of course Khideo would remind everyone of how few men Monush had brought with him. But Monush took no offense. Instead, he raised his hand from his lap and Khideo nodded, giving him the privilege of speech. "As it was, if the enemy had not been made stupid by the power of the Keeper, we would have been caught." Even as he said the formulaic words, he wondered if perhaps they might not be true, at least in this case. Why hadn't any of the Elemaki looked up at one of the many times when Monush's men would have been visible moving across the face of the mountains?

"Now we propose to win the freedom of our whole people," said Khideo. "You know at this table that I do not shrink from battle. You know that I don't think even assassination is beneath my honor."

The others nodded gravely, and now Monush began to suppose that he knew why Khideo had no honorific. It could not have been Ilihiak that he once tried to assassinate—but Nuab must have had some enemies when he was still alive as a truly terrible king. Ilihiak could accept Khideo's counsel and even let him lead his armies, but he could never give an honorific to a man who tried to kill a king—especially his father, as unworthy as the old king might have been.

"Our only hope is to flee from this place," said Khideo. "But to do it, we have to take at least enough of our herds with us to feed us on our journey. Has anyone ever tried to keep turkeys quiet? Will our pigs move as swiftly as a fleeing army needs to move? Not to mention our women and children—the nursing babies, the toddlers—will we take them along the faces of cliffs? March them for half a day or more at top speed?"

"At least the Elemaki know how impossible it is for you to escape as a people," said Monush. "Therefore they post only a few guards here."

"Exactly," said Khideo.

"So we kill them and go!" cried one of the other men.

Khideo did not answer, but waited instead for Ilihiak to gently chide the man and return the voice to Khideo.

"I read again in the record we keep of the history of the Nafari," said Khideo. "When Nafai led his people away from the traitorous lying murderer Elemak and the foul diggers who served him, he had the help of the Keeper of Earth, who made all the Elemaki sleep so soundly that they didn't wake up."

"Nafai was a hero," said an old man. "The Keeper says nothing to us."

"The Keeper spoke to Binaro," said Ilihiak mildly.

"Binadi," muttered another man.

Khideo shook his head. "The Keeper also sent the dream that brought Monush to us. We will trust that after we have done all we can do, the Keeper must do the rest to keep us safe. But my plan does not require us to pray to the Keeper and then hope our prayer is granted. You all know that we are forbidden to ferment any of our barley, even though it makes the water safer from disease. Why is that?"

"Because the beer makes the diggers crazy," said an old man.

"It makes them stupid," said Khideo. "It makes them drunk. Rowdy, noisy, happy, stupid—and then they pass out. This is why we're forbidden to make it—because the dirt-eaters don't have any self-control."

"If we offer them beer," said Ilihiak, "even presuming we can find any—"

Several of the men laughed. Apparently clandestine brewing was not unheard of.

"—what's to stop them from arresting and imprisoning whoever offers it to them?"

Khideo only nodded at the king.

No, not at the king at all. At the king's wife, Wissedwa. She turned her face away, so she didn't look directly at any of the men, but she spoke boldly so all could hear her. "We know that to the diggers all women are sacred. Even if they refuse the beer they will not lay hands on us. So we will offer it to them as the last share of the harvest. They'll know they can't legally turn it in to their superiors without also turning in the criminals who gave it to them; they'll have no choice but to drink it."

"The queen speaks my plan from her own lips," said Khideo.

Monush thought that Khideo bore the shame of deferring to a woman in council with great dignity. He would have to ask, later, why the voice of the woman was heard. In the meantime, though, it was obvious that she was no fool and had followed the discussion completely. Monush tried to imagine a woman at one of Motiak's councils. Who would it be? Not Dudagu, that was certain—had she ever uttered an intelligent word? And Toeledwa, before she died, had always been quiet, refusing even to ask about matters outside the rearing of her children and the affairs of the king's house. But Edhadeya, now— Monush could imagine *her* speaking boldly in council. There'd be no silencing *her* if once she was given the right to speak. This was definitely an idea that should never be suggested to Motiak. He doted on Edhadeya enough that he might just decide to grant her the privilege of speech, and that would be the end of all dignity for the king's council. I have not the humility of this Khideo, thought Monush.

"Now we must know," said Khideo, "whether Monush knows another way back to Darakemba that won't take us through the heart of the land of Nafai."

Monush spoke immediately. "Motiak and I looked at all the maps before my men and I set out. We had no choice but to come up the Tsidorek in search of you, because that was the route of your great king Zenifab when your ancestors left. But for the return, if you know the way to the river Mebberek—"

"It's called Mebbereg in this country," said an old man, "if it's the same river."

"Does it have a tributary with a pure source?" asked Monush.

"Mebbereg's largest tributary is the Ureg. It begins in a lake called Uprod, which is a pure source," said the old man.

"That's the one," said Monush. "There's an ancient pass above Uprod leading into the land northward. I know how to find it, I think, if the land hasn't changed too much since our maps were made. It comes out not far from a bend in the Padurek, which is the great pure-source tributary of the Tsidorek. From the moment we emerge from that pass, we will be in lands ruled by Motiak."

Khideo nodded. "Then we will leave through the back of the city, away from the river. And we'll only need to give the beer to the Elemaki guards who are stationed here in the city. The guards down-river and upriver will never hear us, nor will the ones crossriver know anything is going on. And when the guards discover us gone, they won't dare go to their king to report their failure, because they know that they'll all be slaughtered. Instead they'll flee into the forest themselves and become outlaws and vagabonds, and it will be many days before the king of the Elemaki knows what we've done. That is my plan, O king, and now I return your voice to you."

"I receive back my voice," said Ilihiak. "And I declare that it truly *was* my voice, and Khideo is now my hands and my feet in leading this nation to freedom. He will set the day, and all will obey him as if he were king until we are at the shores of the Mebbereg."

Monush watched as all the other men in the council immediately knelt and touched their palms to the floor, doing obeisance to Khideo. Monush nodded toward him, as befitted the dignity of the emissary of Motiak. Khideo looked at him under a raised eyebrow. Monush didn't let his benign expression waver. After a moment, Khideo must have decided that Monush's nod was enough, for he raised his hands to release the others, and then knelt himself before the king, putting his face between the king's knees and his hands flat on the king's feet.

"Maybe if I could bear my life as it is for one day, for one hour, for one *minute*, I could forget my wish to be something else," Mon finally answered.

Bego turned to him, his gaze softening. "What is this? Honesty, from Mon?"

"I never lie."

"I mean honesty about how you feel."

"Are you going to pretend that it was *my* feelings you were worried about?"

Bego laughed. "I don't worry much about *anybody's* feelings. But yours might matter." He looked at Mon as if he was listening. For what? Mon's heartbeat? For his secret thoughts? I have no secret thoughts, thought Mon. Or rather, they're not secret because I've withheld them—if they're unknown, it's because no one asked.

"Let me lay out a problem for you, Mon," said Bego.

"Back to work," said Mon.

"*My* work this time, not yours."

Mon didn't know whether he was being patronized or respected. So he listened.

"When the Zenifi came back several months ago—you remember?"

"I remember," said Mon. "They were settled in their new land only Ilihiak refused to be their king. He had them choose a governor. The people themselves. And then they showed their ingratitude by choosing Khideo instead of Ilihiak."

"So you *have* been paying attention."

"Was that all?" asked Mon.

"Not at all. You see, when the voice of the people went against Ilihiak, he came here."

"To ask for help? Did he really think Father would impose him as judge on the Zenifi? Ilihiak was the one who decided to let the people vote—let him live with what they voted for!"

"Exactly right, Mon," said Bego, "but of course Ilihiak would be the first to agree with you. He didn't come here in order to *get* power. He came because he was finally *free* of it."

"So he's an ordinary citizen," said Mon. "What was his business with the king?"

"He doesn't need to have business, you know," said Bego. "Your father took a liking to him. They became friends."

127

Mon felt a stab of jealousy. This stranger who had never even known Father's name till Monush found him six months ago was Father's friend, while Mon languished as a mere second son, lucky to see his father once a week on any basis more personal than the king's council.

"But he *did* have business," said Bego. "It seems that after Ilihiak's father was murdered—"

"A nation of regicides—and now they've elected a would-have-been regicide as their governor."

"Yes yes," said Bego impatiently. "Now it's time to listen. After Nuab was murdered and Ilihidis became king—"

"Dis-Ilihi? Not the heir?"

"The people chose the only one of Nuab's sons who hadn't run away when the Elemaki invaded. The only one with any courage."

Mon nodded. He hadn't heard about that. A second son inheriting on the basis of his merit.

"Don't have any fantasies about *that*," said Bego. "Your older brother is no coward. And it ill becomes you to wish for him to be deprived of his inheritance."

Mon leapt to his feet in fury. "How dare you accuse me of thinking any such thing!"

"What second son *doesn't* think it?"

"As well I might assume that *you're* jealous of bGo's great responsibilities, while you're only a librarian and a tutor for children!"

It was Bego's turn to be furious. "How dare you, a mere human, speak of my otherself as if you could compare your feeble brotherhood with the bonds between otherselves!"

They stood there, eye to eye. For the first time, Mon realized, eye to eye with Bego meant that Mon was looking down. His adult height was beginning to come. How had he not noticed till now? A tiny smile came to his lips.

"So, you smile," said Bego. "Why, because you succeeded in provoking me?"

Rather than confess the childish and selfish thought that had prompted his smile, Mon invented another reason, one which became true enough as soon as he thought of it. "Can a student not smile when he provokes his teacher into acting like a child?"

"And I was going to talk to you about genuine matters of state."

"Yes, you were," said Mon. "Only you chose to start by accusing me of wishing for my brother to lose his inheritance."

"For that I apologize."

"I wish you would apologize for calling me a 'mere human,' " said Mon.

"For that I also apologize," said Bego stiffly. "Just because you are a mere human doesn't mean that you can't have meaningful affection and loyalty between siblings. It isn't your fault that you cannot begin to comprehend the bonds of shared selfhood between otherselves among the sky people."

"Ah, Bego, now I understand what Husu meant, when he said that you were the only man he knew who could insult someone worse with your apologies than with your slanders."

"Husu said that?" asked Bego mildly. "And here I thought he hadn't understood me."

"Tell me the business of state," said Mon. "Tell me what business brought Ilihiak to Father."

Bego grinned. "I *thought* you wouldn't be able to resist the story."

Mon waited. When Bego didn't go on, Mon roared with frustration and ran once around the desk, for all the world like a digger child circling a tree before climbing it. He knew he looked silly, but he couldn't *stand* the malicious little games that Bego played.

"Oh, sit down," said Bego. "What Ilihiak came for was to give your father twenty-four leaves of gold."

"Oh," said Mon, disappointed. "Just money."

"Not money at all," said Bego. "There was writing on them. Twenty-four leaves of ancient writing."

"Ancient? You mean, before the Zenifi?"

"Perhaps," said Bego with a faint smile. "Perhaps before the Nafari."

"So there might have been a group of diggers or angels who knew how to work metal? Who knew how to write?"

Bego gave that rippling of his wings that among the angels meant the same as a shrug. "I don't know," said Bego. "I can't read the language."

"But you speak skyspeech and dirtwords and—"

"Earthspeech," Bego corrected him. "Your father doesn't like us to use such disparaging terms toward the earth people."

129

Mon rolled his eyes. "It's an ugly language that barely qualifies as talk."

"Your father rules over a kingdom that includes diggers as citizens."

"Not many. Most of them are slaves. It's in their nature. Even among the Elemaki, humans usually rule over them."

"Usually but not always," said Bego. "And it's good to remember, when disparaging the diggers, to remember that these supposed 'natural slaves' managed to drive our ancestors out of the land of Nafai."

Mon almost jumped into another argument about whether great-grandfather Motiab led his people to Darakemba voluntarily or because they were in danger of being destroyed back in their ancient homeland. But then he realized that this was exactly what Bego wanted him to do. So he sat patiently and waited.

Bego nodded. "So, you refused to take up the distraction. Very good."

Mon rolled his eyes. "You're the teacher, you're the master, you know everything, I am your puppet," he intoned.

Bego had heard this litany of sarcasm before. "And don't you forget it," he said—as he usually did. "Now, these records were found by a party Ilihiak had sent out to look for Darakemba. Only they followed the Issibek instead of the Tsidorek, and then had the bad luck to follow some difficult high valleys until they came out of the gornaya altogether, far to the north of here, in the desert."

"Opustoshen," said Mon, by reflex.

"Another point for knowing geography," said Bego. "What they found, though, was a place we've never found—mostly because it's considerably west of Bodika, and our spies just don't fly that far. Why should they? There's no water there—no enemy can come against us from that quarter."

"So they found the book of gold in the desert?"

"Not a book. Unbound leaves. But it wasn't just a desert. It was the scene of a terrible battle. Vast numbers of skeletons, with armor and weapons cluttered around them where they fell. Thousands and thousands and thousands of soldiers fought there and died."

Bego paused, waiting for something.

And then Mon made the connection. "Coriantumr," he murmured.

Bego nodded his approval. "The legendary man who came to Darakemba as the first human the sky people here had ever seen. We always assumed that he was the survivor of some battle between an obscure group of Nafari or Elemaki somewhere, when humans were first spreading through the gornaya. It was a difficult time, and we lost track of many groups. When the original sky people of Darakemba told us he was the last survivor of a huge war between great nations, we assumed it was just exaggeration. The only thing that stuck in *my* craw, anyway, was the inscription."

Mon had seen it, the large round stone that still stood in the central market of the city. No one had any idea what the inscription meant; they always assumed that it was a sort of primitive imitation of writing that the Darakembi angels came up with, after they heard that humans could write things down and before they learned how to do it themselves."

"So tell me!" Mon demanded. "Is the language on Ilihiak's leaves the same?"

"The Darakembi said that Coriantumr scratched in the dirt to show them what to chisel into the stone. It was slow work, and he was dead before they finished, but they sculpted it first in clay so that they wouldn't forget while they did the slow work of cutting it in stone." Bego dropped from his teaching perch and pulled several waxed barks from a box. "I made a reasonable copy here. How does it look to you?"

Mon looked at the round inscription, wheels within wheels, all with strange twisted pictures on them. "It looks like the Coriantumr stone," he said.

"No, Mon. *This* is the Coriantumr stone." Bego handed him another bark, and this time the image scratched into the wax was identical to the stone as he remembered it.

"So what's the other?"

"A circular inscription on one of the gold leaves."

Mon hooted in appreciation—and noticed, to his chagrin, that he could no longer hoot as high as an angel. It sounded silly to hoot in a man's low voice.

"So the answer to your question is, Yes, Mon, the languages seem to be the same. The problem is that there is no known analogue to this writing system. It clearly does *not* lend itself to decoding in any pattern we can think of."

"But all human languages are based on the language of the Nafari,

131

from them. But there was more food here than they needed anyway. Enough and to spare.

That is the gift the Keeper gave to us: Instead of remaining in fear and loathing as we were, my wife's courage and wisdom turned our worst enemies, the children of Pabulog, into friends. They will not rebel against their father, of course—they're too young and Pabulog too cruel and unpredictable for that. But they've given us peace. And surely even Pabulog will be able to see that it's better to have Akmaro's people as productive serfs than as bitter, resentful, tormented slaves.

The only dark place in the scene that Akmaro surveyed was his son, Akma. Akmadis, Kmadadis, beloved of my heart, my hopes are in you as your mother's hopes are in her sweet daughter. Why have you come to hate me so much? You're clever and wise in your heart, Akma, you can see that it's better to forgive and make friends out of enemies. What is the cause of all this bitterness that makes you so blind? I speak to you and you hear nothing. Or worse—you act as if my voice were the warcry of an enemy in your ears.

Chebeya had comforted him, of course, assuring him that even though the hostility was real enough, the ties between father and son were, if anything, stronger than ever. "You're the center of his life, Kmadaro," she told him. "He's angry now, he thinks he hates you, but in fact he's in orbit around you like the Moon around the Earth."

Small comfort, to face his son's hatred when he wanted—when he deserved!—only love, and had given only love.

But . . . that was Akmaro's personal tragedy, his personal burden, to have lost the love of his son. In time that would get better, or it would not get better; as long as Akmaro did his best, it was out of his hands. Most important was the work he was doing in the cause of the Keeper. He had thought, when he first fled from the knives of Nuak's assassins, that the Keeper had a great work in mind for him. That Binaro's words had been entrusted to him, and he must teach them far and wide. Teach that the Keeper of Earth meant for the people of sky, earth, and all between to live as sisters and brothers, family and friends, with no one master over another, with no rich or poor, but all equal partakers of the land the Keeper had given them, with all people keeping the covenants they made with each other, raising their families in safety and peace, and neither hunger or pride

151

to shame the happiness of anyone. Oh, yes, Akmaro had visions of whole kingdoms awakening to the simplicity of the message the Keeper had given to Binaro, and through him to Akmaro, and through him to all the world.

Instead, his message had been given to these nearly five hundred souls, humans every one of them. And the four sons of Pabulog.

But it was enough, wasn't it? They had proven their courage, these five hundred. They had proven their loyalty and strength. They had borne all things, and they would yet be able to bear many things. That was a good thing that they had created together—this community was a good thing. And when it came to a battle with their most evil enemy, Pabulog, a man even richer in hatred than he was in money and power, Pabulog had won the part with swords and whips, but Akmaro—no, Akmaro's community—no, the Keeper's people—had won the battle of hearts and minds, and won the friendship of Pabulog's sons.

They were good boys, once they learned, once they were taught. They would have the courage to remain good men, despite their father. If I have lost one son—I don't know how—then at least I have gained these four ur-sons, who should have been the inheritance of another man if he hadn't lost them by trying to use them for evil ends.

Perhaps this is the price I pay for winning the Pabulogi: I take away Pabulog's boys, and in return I must give up my own.

A voice of anguish inside him cried out: No, it isn't worth the price, I would trade all the Pabulogi, all the boys in the world, for one more day in which Akmadis looks in my face with the pride and love that he once had for me!

But he didn't mean that. It wasn't a plea, he didn't want the Keeper to think he was ungrateful. Yes, Keeper, I want my son back. But not at the price of anyone else's goodness. Better to lose my son than for you to lose this people.

If only he could believe that he meant that with his whole heart.

"Akmaro."

Akmaro turned and saw Didul standing there. "I didn't hear you come up."

"I ran, but in the breeze perhaps you didn't hear my footfalls."

"What can I do for you?"

Didul looked upset. "It was a dream I had last night."

"What was the dream?" asked Akmaro.

"It was . . . perhaps nothing. That's why I said nothing until now. But . . . I couldn't get it off my mind. It kept coming back and back and back and so I came to tell you."

"Tell me."

"I saw Father arrive. With five hundred Elemaki warriors, some middle people, most of them earth people. He meant to . . . he meant to come upon you at dawn, to take you in your sleep, slaughter you all. Now that the fields are ready to harvest. He had a season of labor from you, and then he was going to slaughter your people before your eyes, and then your wife in front of your children, and then your children in front of you, and you last of all."

"And you waited to tell me this until now?"

"Because even though I saw that this was his plan, even though I saw the scene as he imagined it, when he arrived here he found the place empty. All the potatoes still in the ground, and all of you gone. Not a trace. The guards were asleep, and he couldn't waken them, so he killed them in their sleep and then raced off trying to find you in the forest but you were gone."

Akmaro thought about this for a moment. "And where were you?"

"Me? What do you mean?"

"In your dream. Where were you and your brothers?"

"I don't know. I didn't see us."

"Then . . . don't you think that makes it obvious where you were?"

Didul looked away. "I'm not ashamed to face Father after what we've done here. This was the right way to use the authority he gave us."

"Why didn't he find you here in your dream?"

"Does a son betray his father?" asked Didul.

"If a father commands a son to commit a crime so terrible that the son can't do it and live with himself, then is it betrayal for the son to disobey the father?"

"You always do that," said Didul. "Make all the questions harder."

"I make them truer," said Akmaro.

"Is it a true dream?" asked Didul.

"I think so," said Akmaro.

"How will you get away? The guards are still loyal to Father. They obey us, but they won't let you escape."

"You saw it in the dream. The Keeper did it once before. When

153

the Nafari escaped from the Elemaki, back at the beginning of our time on Earth, the Keeper caused a deep sleep to come upon all the enemies of the Nafari. They slept until the Nafari were safely away."

"You can't be sure that will happen, not from my dream."

"Why not?" asked Akmaro. "We can learn from the dream that your father is coming, but we can't learn from it how the Keeper means to save us?"

Didul laughed nervously. "What if it isn't a true dream?"

"Then the guards will catch us as we leave," said Akmaro. "How will that be worse than waiting for your father to arrive?"

Didul grimaced. "I'm not Binaro. I'm not *you*. I'm not Chebeya. People don't risk their lives because of a dream of mine."

"Don't worry. They'll be risking their lives because they believe in the Keeper."

Didul shook his head. "It's too much. Too much to decide just on the basis of my dream."

Akmaro laughed. "If your dream came out of nowhere, Didul, then no one would care what you dreamed." He touched Didul's shoulder. "Go tell your brothers that I tell them to think about the fact that in your dream, your father doesn't find you here. It's your choice. But I tell you this. If the Keeper thinks you are the enemy of my people, then in the dark hours of morning you'll be asleep when we leave. So if you awaken as we're leaving, the Keeper is inviting you to come. The Keeper is telling you that you are trusted and you belong with us."

"Or else I have a full bladder and have to get up early to relieve myself."

Akmaro laughed again, then turned away from him. The boy would tell his brothers. They would decide. It was between them and the Keeper.

Almost at once, Akmaro saw his son Akma standing in the field, sweaty from harvesting the potatoes. The boy was looking at him. Looking at Didul as he walked away. What did it look like in Akma's eyes? My touching Didul's shoulder. My laughter. What did that look like? And when I tell the people tonight of Didul's dream, tell them to prepare because the voice of the Keeper has come to us, telling us that tomorrow we will be delivered out of bondage—when I tell them that, the others will rejoice because the Keeper has not forsaken us. But my son will rage in his heart because the dream came to Didul, and not to him.

The afternoon passed; the sun, long since hidden behind the mountains, now at last withdrew its light from the sky. Akmaro gathered the people and told them to prepare, for in the hours before dawn they would depart. He told them of the dream. He told them who dreamed it. And no one raised a doubt or a question. No one said, "Is it a trap? Is it a trick?" Because they all knew the Pabulogi, knew how they had changed.

In the early morning, Akmaro and Chebeya awoke their children. Then Akmaro went out to make sure all the others were awake and preparing to go. They would send no one to spy on the guards. They knew they were either asleep—or not. There was no reason to check, nothing they could do if they had interpreted the dream wrongly.

Inside the hut, as Akma helped fill their traveling bags with the food they would need to carry and the spare clothing and tools and ropes they'd need, Mother spoke to him. "It wasn't Didul, you know. He didn't choose to have the dream, and your father didn't choose to hear it from him. It was the Keeper."

"I know," said Akma.

"It's the Keeper trying to teach you to accept her gifts no matter whom she chooses to give them through. It's the Keeper who wants you to forgive. They're not the same boys they were when they tormented you. They've asked for your forgiveness."

Akma paused in his work and looked her in the eye. Without rancor—without any kind of readable expression—he said, "They've asked, but I refuse."

"I think it's beneath you now, Akma. I could understand it at first. The hurt was still fresh."

"You don't understand," said Akma.

"I know I don't. That's why I'm begging you to explain it to me."

"I didn't forgive them. There was nothing to forgive."

"What do you mean?"

"They were doing as their father taught them. I was doing as my father taught me. That's all. Children are nothing but tools of their parents."

"Basilica is the name of the fixed star," said Bego, "and Harmony is the name of the planet orbiting that star."

"Say the scholars," said Akma. "Who know nothing more than we do, since they reach all their conclusions from the same records. And I say the record of the Heroes is obviously wrong. There *were* people here, the Rasulum."

Bego shrugged. "That has caused a little consternation among the scholars."

"Come on," said Mon. "That's the very fact you keep throwing in our faces every time we discuss history. You want us to discover something from it so don't play innocent now."

Akma went on. "What if humans never left this world at all? What if humans were simply forced to stay away from the gornaya during the era when it was being lifted up by volcanos and earthquakes? The Heroes talk of how there was once a time when the land masses were getting folded into each other and raised high, the tallest mountains in the world. So what if *that* was what gave rise to the legend of the dispersal? No humans in the gornaya, therefore no humans in the world—but actually humans to the north, in the prairie lands. Then there's a terrible war, and as many humans as can, flee from the Rasulum. Some of them brave the old tabus and come into the gornaya. Perhaps they even come by boat, but they're afraid the gods they worship—the Oversoul and the Keeper of Earth—will be angry at them for doing it, so they talk of having come from the stars instead of from Opustoshen."

"Then why is the language of the leaves so different from our language?" asked Bego.

"Because it hasn't been a mere four hundred or five hundred years since the time of the Heroes. In fact they split off from the Rasulum a thousand years ago, perhaps more. And the languages grew more and more different, until nothing was alike."

"And what does that have to do with angels and diggers?" asked Bego.

"Nothing at all!" cried Mon. "Don't you see? The humans came and dominated everybody, and forced their gods on everybody. But didn't the diggers worship gods that the angels made for them? And didn't the angels have their own gods to worship? None of this Keeper nonsense. The angels and diggers evolved separately here

173

in the gornaya while the humans stayed away in the land north-ward."

"What about the stories of Shedemei discovering some strange organ in all the sky people and all the earth people that forced us to remain together?" asked Bego.

"The story says that she caused you all to get sick and it made those organs disappear from your children," said Akma. "So now, conveniently enough, there's not a lick of evidence left that those organs ever existed."

"All the stories use for evidence things that can't be checked now," said Mon. "That's a standard rhetorical trick—one that any fool can expose in a public debate or trial. The new star in the sky is Basilica—but how do we know that star wasn't there all along?"

"The records are ambiguous about that," said Bego.

"The only evidence we *do* have," said Akma, "is a flat contradiction of the records of the Heroes. They said there were no other humans on Earth when they arrived. But we have the bones of Opustoshen and the leaves of the Rasulum to prove otherwise. Don't you see? The only evidence denies everything."

Bego looked at them placidly. "Well, this certainly is treasonous," he finally said.

"But it doesn't have to be," said Akma. "That's what I've been explaining to Mon. His father's authority comes from being a direct descendant of the first Nafai. That part of the record isn't being questioned. The kingdom is not challenged."

"No," said Bego. "Only your father is challenged."

Akma smiled. "If my father is teaching people to behave in uncomfortable ways, solely because the Keeper says they must, and then it turns out there is no Keeper, then whose will *is* it that my father is trying to foist onto the people?"

"I think your father is a sincere man," said Bego.

"Sincere but wrong," said Akma. "And the people hate what he's teaching."

"The former slaves love it," said Bego.

"The *people*," said Akma.

"I gather, then, that you don't consider diggers to be people," said Bego.

"I consider them to be the natural enemies of humans and angels.

174

And I also think that there's no reason why humans should rule over angels."

"Now we're definitely back to treason," said Bego.

"Why not an alliance?" said Mon. "A king of the humans and a king of the angels, both ruling over peoples spread through the same territory?"

"Not possible," said Bego. "One king for one territory. Otherwise there would be war and hatred between humans and angels. The Elemaki would seize the opportunity and destroy us all."

"But we shouldn't be required to live together, anyway," said Akma.

Bego looked at Mon. "Is that what you want?" he asked. "You, who as a child dreamed of being—"

"My childish dreams are done with!" Mon cried. "In fact if I hadn't been living among angels I wouldn't have had those wishes, would I!"

"I thought they were rather sweet. And perhaps a bit flattering," said Bego. "Considering how many angels grow up wishing they were human."

"None!" cried Mon. "Not one!"

"Many."

"They're all mad, then," Mon replied.

"Quite likely," said Bego. "So let's see if I understand you. There is no Keeper and there never was. Humans never left Earth, just the gornaya. Diggers and angels never needed each other and there was no tiny organ that Shedemei removed from our bodies with a disease. And therefore there is no reason to change our whole way of life, all our customs, just because Akmaro tells us that it's the will of the Keeper that the three species become one people, the Keeper's Children, the People of Earth."

"Exactly," said Akma.

"So what?" asked Bego.

Akma and Mon looked at each other. "What do you mean, so what?" asked Mon.

"So why are you telling me?" asked Bego.

"Because maybe you can talk to Father about this," said Mon. "Get him to stop pushing these laws."

"Take my father away from his position of authority," said Akma.

175

Bego blinked once at Akma's words. "If I said these things to your father, my dear friends, I would simply be removed immediately from any position of responsibility. That's the *only* change that would be made."

"Does my father completely control the king, then?" asked Akma.

"Careful," said Mon. "Nobody controls my father."

"You know what I mean," Akma said impatiently.

"And I know Motiak," said Bego. "He's not going to change his mind, because as far as he's concerned, you have no evidence at all. For him, the very fact that true dreams led the soldiers of Ilihiak to find the Rasulum leaves is proof that the Keeper wanted them found. Therefore it is the Keeper who corrects the mistakes of the Heroes— more proof that the Keeper lived then, and the Keeper lives now. You aren't going to dissuade someone who wants so desperately to believe in the Keeper."

Angrily, Akma pound his fist down into the sod. "My father *must* be stopped from spreading his lies!"

"His mistakes," said Bego. "Remember? You would never be so disloyal a son as to accuse your father of lying. Who would believe you then?"

"Just because he believes them doesn't mean they're not lies," said Akma.

"Ah, but they're not *his* lies, are they?" said Bego. "So you must call them mistakes, when you say they are your father's."

Mon chuckled. "Do you hear him, Akma? He's with us. This is what he wanted us to realize all along."

"Why do you think so?" asked Bego.

"Because you're advising us on strategy," said Mon.

Akma sat up, grinning. "Yes, you are, aren't you, Bego!"

Bego shrugged again. "You can't possibly have any strategy right now. Akmaro is too closely linked to the king's policy, and vice versa. But perhaps there'll come a time when the Houses of the Kept are much more clearly separated from the house of the king."

"What do you mean?" asked Akma.

"I mean only this. There are those who want to tear your father from his throne, they're so angry about these policies."

"That's not what we want!" cried Mon.

"Of course not. No one in their right mind wants that. The only reason we don't have invasions from the Elemaki every year is because the entire empire of Darakemba is united, with armies and spies constantly patrolling and protecting our borders. It's only a tiny minority of bigots and madmen who want to throw down the throne. However, that tiny treasonous minority will gain more and more support, the farther your father pushes these reforms of Akmaro's. It will mean civil war, sooner or later, and no matter who wins, we'll be weakened. There are people who don't want that. Who want us to go back to the way we were before."

"The old priests, you mean," said Mon scornfully.

"Some of them, yes," said Bego.

"And you," said Akma. "You want things to go back the way they were."

"I don't have opinions on public policy," said Bego. "I'm a scholar, and I'm reporting to you in a scholarly way the current condition of the kingdom. There are those who want to fend off civil war, protect the throne, and stop Akmaro from pushing these insane, offensive, impossible laws breaking down all distinctions between men and women, humans and diggers and angels. All this talk of forgiveness and understanding."

Akma interrupted, full of bitterness. "It's only a mask for those who want to turn this into a land where diggers strut around with weapons in their hands, tormenting their betters and—"

"You almost make me fear that you are one of those who wants to destroy this kingdom," said Bego. "If that is the case, Akma, then you'll be of no use to those who are trying to preserve the throne."

Akma fell silent, pulling at the grass. A clump came free, spraying his face with dirt. Angrily he brushed it away.

"But what if those who are trying to preserve the throne could assure the people, Just wait. The children of Motiak don't believe in this nonsense of all the species being equal children of the Keeper. The children of Akma have no intention of pursuing their father's mad policies. Be patient. When the time comes, things will go back to the old way."

"I'm not the heir," said Mon.

"Then perhaps you should work to persuade Aronha," said Bego.

"Even if I did, Father would only pass the kingdom on to Ominer, skipping us both."

"Was I really right all those times?" asked Mon. "Or were you simply as eager as I was to believe that children our age could actually know something?"

Wrong. This is wrong. This is wrong.

Mon kept his face expressionless—he hoped.

Aronha smiled half-heartedly. "Go get Akma," he said to Mon. "If I know him at all, he's not far off. Waiting for one of us to go and get him. You do it, Mon. Bring him back. We'll be united with him. For the good of the kingdom."

Khideo greeted Ilihiak with an embrace. No, not Ilihiak. Ilihi. A man who was once a king, now insisting that there was nothing extraordinary about him, that he had not been touched by the hand of the Keeper. It seemed so odd, so much like a kind of failure. But not Ilihi's failure, really. More as if the universe itself had failed.

"And how is the—how is your wife?" asked Khideo.

The normal meaningless greetings took only a few moments; they were made all the more brief because Khideo's wife had died many years before, in trying to give birth to their first child. It would have been a boy. The midwife said that the child was so big, like his father, that the head tore her apart passing through the channel of life. Khideo knew then that he had killed his wife, because any child of his would be too large for a woman to bear. The Keeper meant him to be childless; but at least Khideo didn't have to kill any more women trying to defy the Keeper's will. So Ilihi, who knew all this, made no inquiries about family.

"The weight of government rests lightly on you, Khideo."

Khideo laughed. Or meant to laugh. It came out as a dry sound in his throat. He coughed. "I feel my muscles slackening. The soldier I once was is becoming soft and old. I'm drying out from the inside. At least I won't be one of those fat old men. Instead I'll be frail."

"I won't live to see it!"

"I'm older than you, Ilihi; you'll see me dead, I can assure you. A wind will come from the east, a terrible hurricane, and it will blow me up over the mountains and out into the ocean but I'll be so dry that I'll just float there on the surface like a leaf until the sun dries me to powder and I finally dissolve."

Ilihi looked at him with such a strange expression that Khideo had to shove him gently in the shoulder, the way he had done when Ilihi was Nuak's third and least favored son and Khideo took pity on him and taught him what it meant to be a man and a soldier. They had been together the day that Khideo finally had enough. The day he took his vow to kill the king. He had shoved him gently, just like this, and had seen tears come to Ilihi's eyes. Khideo asked him then what was wrong, and Ilihi broke down and wept and told him what Pabulog had been doing to him since he was a little child. "It's been years since he did it last," said Ilihi. "I'm married now. I have a daughter. I thought it was over. But he took me out of my father's presence at breakfast and did it to me again. Two of his guards held me while he did it." Khideo went numb when he heard this. "Your father doesn't know what use Pabulog made of you, does he?" And Ilihi told him, "Of course he knows. I told him. He said that it only happened to me because I was weak. The Keeper intended me to be born a girl."

Khideo knew of many terrible things that had gone wrong in the kingdom of Nuak. He had seethed watching how Nuak mistreated the people around him, how he tolerated unspeakable vices among his closest associates, how only a few decent men were left among the leaders of the kingdom—but still there were those few, and Nuak was the king. But this was more than Khideo could bear. King or no king, no man could let such a thing happen to his son and not strike down the man who did it. In Khideo's eyes, it was not his own place to kill Pabulog—that was for Nuak to do, or failing that for Ilihi to do when he finally found his tortured way to manhood. But Khideo was a soldier, sworn to protect the throne and the people from all enemies. He knew who the enemy was now. It was Nuak. Strike him down, and all these others would fall, too. So he made his vow that the king would die by his hands. He had him under his hands at the top of the tower, ready to eviscerate him with his short sword as one kills a cowardly enemy, when Nuak looked around and saw, in the borders of the land, a huge army of Elemaki coming to attack. "You have to let me live, so I can lead the defense of our people!" Nuak demanded, and Khideo, who had only been acting for the people's good, saw that Nuak was right.

Then Nuak had led the full retreat of the whole army, leaving only a handful of brave men to defend all the women and children. Off in the wilderness, it was the men he had led in cowardly retreat who tortured him to death. And in the city, Khideo had had to bear the humiliation of letting Ilihi's wife lead the young girls forward to plead for the lives of the people, because there weren't swords enough to hold the Elemaki back for even a moment.

All of this was in the back of Khideo's mind whenever he was with Ilihi. He had seen this boy at his weakest. He had seen him turn into a man and lead a kingdom. But the damage had been done. Ilihi was still broken. Why else would he have set aside the throne?

Yet, having heard Khideo's playful thanatopsis—he meant it to be playful—Ilihi looked at him with strange concern. "You sound as if you long for death, but I know it's not true," said Ilihi.

"I long for death, Ilihi," said Khideo. "Just not mine."

Then the two of them burst into laughter.

"Ah, Lihida, my old friend, I should have been your father."

"Khideo, believe me, except in the biological sense, you were. You are."

"So have you come to me for fatherly counsel?" asked Khideo.

"My wife has heard rumors," said Ilihi.

Khideo rolled his eyes.

"Yes, well, she knows you wouldn't want to hear it from her, but as soon as I told you what we heard, you'd know it came from her. No *man* would tell this to *me*."

It was well known that Ilihi had rejected the Zenifi's absolute refusal to live with the sky people. It was well known that in his own home, angels visited often and were his friends. That was why no man of the land of Khideo would have spoken of secret things to Ilihi. He could not be trusted.

With the women it was different. Men couldn't control their wives, it was that simple. They *would* talk. And they didn't have sense to know who could be trusted and who could not. Ilihi and his wife were good, decent people. But when it came to protecting the Zenifi way of life—the *human* way of life—Ilihi simply should not be taken into confidence. Except that Khideo would never lie to Ilihi. If Ilihi wanted to hear whether the rumors were true, he knew he could come to the governor of the land of Khideo.

"The rumors?"

"She hears that some highly placed men of the land of Khideo are boasting that the son of Akmaro and the sons of the king have become Zenifi in their hearts."

"Not true," said Khideo. "I can assure you that not even the most optimistic among us has any hope of that group of young men declaring that they think angels and humans should not live together."

Ilihi took that in silence and ruminated on it for a while.

"So tell me what that group of young men *will* declare?" asked Ilihi.

"Maybe nothing," said Khideo. "How should I know?"

"Don't lie to me, Khideo. Don't start lying to me now."

"I'm not lying. I should knock you down for accusing me of it."

"What, the man who thinks he's dry as a dead leaf, knock me down?"

"There are stories," said Khideo.

"Meaning that you have a single reliable source that you trust implicitly."

"Why can't it just be stories and rumors?"

"Because, Khideo, I know the way you gather intelligence. You would never consent to be governor of this place if you didn't have a highly placed friend in Motiak's council."

"How would I get such a friend, Ilihi? All those surrounding the king have been with him forever—since long before *we* got here. In fact, *you're* the only man I know who's a friend of Motiak."

Ilihi looked at him narrowly, and thought about that for a while, too. Then he smiled. Then he laughed. "You sly old spy," he said.

"Me?"

"You pure-hearted Zenifi, you rigid upholder of the law of separation, no *man* in the king's council is talking to you. Now, that could mean your informant is a woman, but I think not, mostly because during your brief time in the capital you managed to offend every highly-placed woman who might have helped you. So that means your informant must be an angel."

Khideo shook his head, saying nothing. People underestimated Ilihi. They always had. And even though Khideo knew better, he still managed to be surprised when Ilihi took only the slightest evidence and ran with it straight to the right conclusion.

"So you have struck an alliance with an angel," said Ilihi.

"Not an alliance."

"You find each other useful."

Khideo nodded. "Possibly."

"Akma and the sons of Motiak, they *are* plotting something."

"Not treason," said Khideo. "They would never act to weaken the power of the throne. Nor would Motiak's sons ever do anything to harm him."

"But you don't want to see Motiak brought down, anyway," said Ilihi. "Not you, not any of the Zenifi. No, you're content with this arrangement, living here in these boggy lands—"

"Content? Every bit of soil we farm has to be dug up from the muck and carried here to raise the land above the flood. We have to wall it with logs and stones—which we have to float down from higher lands—"

"You're still in the gornaya."

"Flat, that's what this land is. Flat and boggy."

"You're content," said Ilihi, "because you have the protection of Motiak's armies keeping the Elemaki from you, while Motiak allows you to live without angels in your sky."

"They're in our sky all the time. But they don't live among us. We don't hurt them, they don't bother us."

"Akmaro is your problem, isn't he. Teaching the things Binaro taught."

"Binadi," said Khideo.

"Binaro, who said that the great evil of the Zenifi was to reject not just the angels, but the diggers as well. That the Keeper would not be happy with us until in every village in all the world, human, digger, and angel lived together in harmony. Then in that day the Keeper would come to Earth in the shape of a human, a digger, and an angel, and—"

"No!" Khideo cried out in rage, lashing out with his hand. If the blow had landed on Ilihi it would have knocked him down, for the truth was that Khideo had lost very little of his great strength. But Khideo slapped at nothing, at air, at an invisible inaudible mosquito. "Don't remind me of the things he said."

"Your anger is still a fearsome thing, Khideo."

"Binaro should have been killed before he converted Akmaro. Nuak waited too long, that's what I think."

"I expected you to jab me the way you used to when you were a brat."

"So I've passed out of brathood."

"Now you judge me," said Akma. "Not because I'm wrong, but because I'm not loyal to Father."

"Aren't you loyal to him?"

"Was he ever loyal to me?" asked Akma.

"And will you ever grow out of the hurts of your childhood?"

Akma got a distant look on his face. "I've grown out of all the hurts that ended."

"No one's hurting you now," said Luet. "You're the one who hurts Mother and Father."

"I'm sorry to hurt Mother," said Akma. "But she made her choice."

"Didul and Pabul and Udad and Muwu all begged for our forgiveness. I forgave them then, and I still forgive them now. They've become decent men, all of them."

"Yes, you all forgave them."

"Yes," said Luet. "You say that as if there were something wrong with it."

"You had the right to forgive them for what they did to you, Luet. But you didn't have the right to forgive them for what they did to me."

Luet remembered seeing Akma alone on a hillside, watching as Father taught the people, with the Pabulogi seated in the front row. "Is that what this is all about? That Father forgave them without waiting for your consent?"

"Father forgave them before they asked him to," whispered Akma. She could barely hear him above the roaring of the crowd, and then she could only make out his words by watching his lips. "Father loved the ones who tormented me. He loved them more than me. There has never been such a vile, perverted, filthy, unnatural injustice as that."

"It wasn't about justice," said Luet. "It was about teaching. The Pabulogi only knew the moral world their father had created for them. Before they could understand what they were doing, they had to be taught to see things as the Keeper sees them. When they did understand, then they begged forgiveness and changed their ways."

241

"But Father already loved them," whispered Akma. "When they were still beating you, when they were still torturing me, mocking us both, smearing us with digger feces, tripping me and kicking me, stripping me naked and holding me upside down in front of all the people while they ridiculed me—while they were still doing those things, Father already loved them."

"He saw what they could become."

"He had no right to love them more than me."

"His love for them saved all our lives," said Luet.

"Yes, Luet, and look what his love has done for them. They prosper. They're happy. In his eyes, they *are* his sons. Better sons than I am."

This was uncomfortably close to Luet's own judgment of things. "There's nothing they've achieved, nothing in their relationship with Father that wasn't available to you."

"As long as I admitted first that there was no difference in value between the tortured and the torturer."

"That's stupid, Akma," said Luet. "They had to *change* before Father accepted them. They had to become someone else."

"Well, I *haven't* changed," said Akma. "I haven't changed."

It was the most personal conversation Luet had had with Akma in years, and she longed for it to continue, but at that moment a roar went up from the crowd because they were bringing in the accused, protected by eight guards. This was another old tradition, introduced after several cases in which the accused was murdered in court before the trial was even completed, or snatched away to have another sort of trial in another place. These guards still served that practical purpose—an in-court murder of an accused person had happened not ten years before, admittedly in the rather wild provincial capital of Trubi, at the high end of the valley of the Tsidorek. Not that anyone expected Shedemei to be in danger. This was a test case, a struggle for power; she herself was not regarded with particular passion by those accusing her.

"Look at the pride in her," said Akma, shouting right in her ear so he could be heard.

Pride? Yes, but not the cocky sort of defiance that some affected to when haled before the court. She carried herself with simple dignity, looking around her calmly with mild interest, without fear, without shame. Luet had thought that no one could be charged and brought to trial without feeling at least a degree of embarrassment at being made a public spectacle, but Shedemei seemed to be no more emotionally involved than a mildly interested spectator.

And yet this trial did matter to her; hadn't she deliberately provoked it? She wanted this to happen. Did she know what the outcome would be, the way she knew in advance the charges against her?

"Has Father told you what the puppet is supposed to decide?" Akma shouted in her ear.

She ignored him. The guards were moving slowly through the crowded gallery, forcing people to sit down. It would take a while for them to silence the crowd—these people wanted to make noise.

She wanted to personally slap each one of them, because their noise had stopped Akma from baring his soul to her. That *was* what he was doing. For some reason, he had chosen this moment to . . . to what? To make a last plea for her understanding. That's what it was. He was on the verge of some action, some public action. He wanted to justify himself to her. To remind her that Father was the one who had first been guilty of monstrous disloyalty. And why? Because Akma himself was preparing his own monstrous disloyalty. A public betrayal.

Akma was going to testify. He was going to be called as a scholar, an expert on religious teachings among the Nafari. He was certainly qualified, as Bego's star pupil. And even though within the family and the royal house it was well known that Akma no longer believed in the existence of the Keeper, it wouldn't stop him from testifying about what the ancient beliefs and customs had always been.

She laid her hand on Akma's arm, dug into his wrist with her fingers.

"Ow!" he cried, pulling away from her.

She leaned in close to him and shouted in his ear. "Don't do it!"

"Don't do what?" She could make out his words only by reading his lips.

"You can't hurt the Keeper!" she shouted. "You'll only hurt the people who love you!"

He shook his head. He couldn't hear her. He couldn't understand her words.

The crowd at last was quieter. Quieter. Till the last murmur finally died. Luet might have spoken to Akma again, but his attention was entirely on the trial. The moment had passed.

"Who speaks for the accusers?" asked Pabul.

kRo stepped forward. "kRo," he said.

"And who are the accusers?"

Each stepped forward in turn, naming himself. Three humans and two angels, all prominent men—one retired from the army, the others men of business or learning. All well known in the city, though none of them held an office that could be stripped from them in retaliation by an angry king.

"Who speaks for the accused?" asked Pabul.

Shedemei answered in a clear, steady voice, "I speak for myself."

"Who is the accused?" asked Pabul.

"Shedemei."

"Your family is not known here," said Pabul.

"I come from a far city that was destroyed many years ago. My parents and my husband and my children are all dead."

Luet heard this in astonishment. There were no rumors about this in the city; Shedemei must never have spoken of her family before. She had once had a husband and children, and they were dead! Perhaps that explained the quietness that Shedemei seemed to have in the deepest place in her heart. Her real life was already over; she did not fear death, because in a way she was already dead. Her children, gone before her! That was not the way the world should be.

"I wandered for a long time," Shedemei went on, "until finally I found a land of peace, where I could teach whatever children were willing to learn, whose parents were willing to send them."

"Digger-lover!" someone cried out from the gallery.

The time of noise had passed; two guards immediately homed in on the heckler and had him out of the gallery in moments. Outside, someone else would be let in to take his place.

"The court is ready to hear the accusations," said Pabul.

kRo launched at once into a listing of Shedemei's supposed crimes, but not the simple unadorned statements that had been in the book of charges. No, each charge became a story, an essay, a sermon. He built up quite a colorful picture, Luet thought—Shedemei defiling the young human and angel girls of the city by forcing them to associate with the filthy ignorant children of diggers from Rat Creek. Shedemei striking at the ancient teachings of all the priests: "And I will call witnesses who will explain how all her teachings are an offense against the tradition of the Nafari—" that would be Akma, thought Luet.

"She insults the memory of Mother Rasa, wife of the Hero Volemak, the great Wetchik, father of Nafai and Issib. . . .' "

Volemak was also the father of Elemak and Mebbekew, Luet wanted to retort—and Rasa had nothing to do with *their* conception. But of course she held her tongue. That *would* be a scandal, if the daughter of the high priest were to be hustled out of the court for heckling.

". . . by pretending that she needs more honor than her marriage to Volemak already brought her! And to give her this redundant honor, she takes a male honorific, *ro,* which means 'great teacher,' and appends it to a woman's name! Rasaro's House, she calls her school! As if Rasa had been a man! What do her students learn just by walking in her door! That there is no difference between men and women!"

To Luet's—and everyone else's—shock, Shedemei spoke up, interrupting kRo's peroration. "I'm new in your country," she said. "Tell me the female honorific that means 'great teacher' and I'll gladly use that one."

kRo waited for Pabul to rebuke her.

"It is not the custom for the accused to interrupt the accuser," said Pabul mildly.

"Not the custom," said Shedemei. "But not a law, either. And as recently as fifty years ago, in the reign of Motiab, the king's late grandfather, it was frequently the case that the accused could ask for a clarification of a confusing statement by the accuser."

"All my speeches are perfectly clear!" kRo answered testily.

"Shedemei calls upon ancient custom," said Pabul, clearly delighted with her answer. "She asked you a question, kRo, and custom requires you to clarify."

"There *is* no female honorific meaning 'great teacher,' " said kRo.

"So by what title should I honor a woman who was a great teacher?" asked Shedemei. "In order to avoid causing ignorant children to be confused about the differences between men and women."

She said this with an ever-so-slightly ironic tone, making it clear that no honorific could possibly cause confusion on such an obvious point. Some in the gallery laughed a little. This was annoying to kRo; it was outrageous of her to have interrupted his carefully memorized speech, forcing him to make up answers on the spot.

It was too big a jump, from helping out secretly at Rasaro's House to running it. The month she had spent learning medicine from Shedemei hadn't helped prepare her for running a school. Edhadeya knew from the start that "running" the school simply meant tending to the details that no one else felt responsible for. Checking that the doors were locked. Buying needed supplies that no one else noticed were running out. She certainly didn't need to tell any of the other teachers how to do their work.

She taught no students herself. Instead she went from class to class, learning what she could from each teacher, not only about the subjects they taught, but also about their methods. She soon learned that while her tutors had been knowledgeable enough, they had had no understanding about how to teach children. If she had started teaching right away, she would have taught as she had been taught; now, she would begin very differently, and whatever students she might someday have would be far happier because of it.

One duty she kept for herself and no others—she answered the door. Whatever the Unkept might try at this school, it would happen first to the daughter of the king. See then whether the civil guard looks the other way! Several times she answered the door to find unaccountable strangers with the lamest sort of excuse for being there; once there were several others gathered nearby. To her it was obvious that they had been hoping for an opportunity—one of the other teachers, perhaps, or, best of all, a little digger girl they could beat up or humiliate or terrify. They had been warned, though, about Edhadeya, and after a while they seemed to have given up.

Then one day she answered the door to find an older man standing there, one whose face she had once known, but couldn't place at once. Nor did he know her.

"I've come to see the master of the school," he said.

"I'm the acting master these days. If it's Shedemei you want, she should be back soon from the provinces."

He looked disappointed, but still he lingered, not looking at her. "I've come a long way."

"In better times, sir, I would invite you in and offer you water at least, a meal if you would have it. But these are hard times and I don't allow strangers in this school."

He nodded, looked down at the ground. As if he was ashamed. Yes. He was ashamed.

"You seem to feel some personal responsibility for the troubles," she said. "Forgive me if I'm presumptuous."

When he looked at her there were tears swimming in his old eyes under the fierce, bushy eyebrows. It did not make him look soft; if anything, it made him seem more dangerous. But not to her. No, she knew that now—he was not dangerous to her or anyone here. "Come in," she said.

"No, you were right to keep me out," he said. "I came here to see . . . the master . . . because I *am* responsible, partly so, anyway, and I can't think how to make amends."

"Let me give you water, and we can talk. I'm not Shedemei—I don't have her wisdom. But it seems to me that sometimes any interested stranger will do when you need to unburden yourself, as long as you know she'll not use your words to harm you."

"Do I know that?" asked the old man.

"Shedemei trusts me with her school," said Edhadeya. "I have no prouder testimony to my character than that."

He followed her into the school, then into the small room by the door that served Shedemei as an office. "Don't you want to know my name?" he asked.

"I want to know how you think you caused these troubles."

He sighed. "Until three days ago I was a high official in one of the provinces. It won't be hard to guess *which* province when I tell you that there have been no troubles at all there, since no angels live within its borders, and diggers have never been tolerated."

"Khideo," she said, naming the province.

He shuddered.

And then she realized that she had also named the man. "Khideo," she said again, and this time he knew from the tone of her voice that she was naming *him*, and not just the land that had been named after him.

"What do you know of me? A would-be regicide. A bigot who wanted a society of pure humans. Well, there *are* no pure humans, that's what I'm thinking. We talked of a campaign to drive all diggers from Darakemba. But it came to nothing for many years, a way to pass the time, a way to reassure ourselves that we were the noble ones,

268

we *pure* humans, if only the others, the ones who lived among the animals, if only they could understand. I see the disgust in your face, but it's the way I was raised, and if you'd seen diggers the way I saw them, murderous, cruel, whips in their hands—"

"The way diggers in Darakemba have been taught to see humans?"

He nodded. "I never saw it that way until these recent troubles. It got out of hand, you see, when word spread—when I helped spread the word—that inside the king's own house, all four of his possible heirs had rejected the vile species-mixing religion of Akmaro. Not to mention Akmaro's own son, though we had known *he* was one of us for a long time. But all the king's sons—that was like giving these *pure* humans license to do whatever they wanted. Because they knew they would win in the end. They knew that when Motiak passes into being Motiab and Aronha become Aronak. . . ."

"And they started beating children."

"They started with vandalism. Shouting. But soon other stories started coming in, and the pure humans that I knew said, What can we do? The young ones are so ardent in their desire for purity. We tell them not to be mean, but who can contain the anger of the young? At first I thought they meant this; I advised them on ways to reign in the ones doing the beatings. But then I realized that . . . I overheard them when they didn't know that I could hear, laughing about angels with holes in their wings. How does an angel fly with holes in his wings? Much faster, but only in one direction. They laughed at this. And I realized that they weren't trying to stop the violence, they loved it. And I had harbored them. I had provided a haven for the Unkept from other provinces to meet together in the days before Akmaro removed all serious penalties for heresy. Now I have no influence over them at all. I couldn't stop them. All I could do was refuse to pretend I was their leader. I resigned my office as governor and came here to learn. . . ."

"To learn what, Khideo?"

"To learn how to be human. Not *pure* human. But a man like my old friend Akmaro."

"Why didn't you go to him?"

Again tears came to Khideo's eyes. "Because I'm ashamed. I don't know Shedemei. I only hear that she is stern and ruthlessly honest. Well, no, I also heard that she favors the mixing of species and all sort

269

of other abominations. That's how word of her came to my city. My former city. But you see, in these last weeks, it occurred to me that if my friends were loathsome, perhaps I needed to learn from my enemies."

"Shedemei is not your enemy," said Edhadeya.

"I have been *her* enemy, then, until now. I realized that all my loathing for angels had been taught to me from childhood, and I only continued to feel that way because it was the tradition of my people. I actually knew and liked several angels, including one rude old scholar in the king's house."

"Bego," said Edhadeya.

He looked at her in surprise. "But of course he would be better known here in the capital." Then he studied her face and knitted his brow. "Have we met before?"

"Once, long ago. You didn't want to listen to me."

He thought for a moment longer, then looked aghast. "I have been pouring out my heart to the king's daughter," he said.

"Except for Akmaro himself, you couldn't have spoken to anyone gladder to hear these words from you. My father honors you, in spite of his disagreement with you. When you see fit to tell him that those disagreements exist no longer, he will embrace you as a long lost brother. So will Ilihi, and so will Akmaro."

"I didn't want to listen to women," said Khideo. "I didn't want to live with angels. I didn't want diggers to be citizens. Now I have come to a school run by women to learn how to live with angels and diggers. I want to change my heart and I don't know how."

"Wanting to is the whole lesson; all the rest is practice. I will say nothing to my father or anyone else about who you are."

"Why didn't you name yourself to me?"

"Would you have spoken to me then?"

He laughed bitterly. "Of course not."

"And please remember that you also refrained from naming yourself to *me*."

"You guessed soon enough."

"And so did you."

"But *not* soon enough."

"And I say that no harm has been done." She rose from her chair. "You may attend any class, but you must do it in silence. Listen. You

diggers could steal the children of angels and eat them in their dank warrens. One can hardly list that as a qualification for citizenship! Most diggers that live in Darakemba, however, are here because they or their parents took part in a raiding party on the borders of our land, trying to steal from hardworking men and women the fruits of their labors. Either they were captured in bloody battle or were taken when a retaliatory raid captured a digger village; then they were brought here as slaves. That was a mistake! That was wrong! Not because the diggers are not suited to slavery—by nature they *are* slaves, and that is how the rulers of the Elemaki treat them all. No, our mistake was that even as slaves, even as trophies of victory, it was wrong to bring diggers into a nation of people, where some would be deceived. Yes, some would think that because the diggers were capable of a kind of speech, they were therefore capable of thinking like, feeling like, acting like *people*. But we must not be deceived. Our eyes can tell us that these are lies. What human hasn't rejoiced to see an angel in flight or hear the eveningsong of our brothers and sisters! What angel has not delighted in the learning that the humans brought with them, the powerful tools that can be shaped and wielded by strong human arms! We can live together, help each other—though I am not saying that our brothers in Khideo may not continue to deprive themselves of the good company of the sky people if they so choose."

Another appreciative laugh from the audience.

"But do you rejoice to see the buttocks of a digger flash in the air as he burrows into the earth? Do you love to hear their whining, grating voices, to see their claws touching food that you are expected to eat? Isn't it a mockery when you see their spadelike fingers clutching a book? Don't you long to leave the room if one of them should ever attempt to sing?"

Each line of abuse was greeted with a laugh.

"They didn't choose to live among us! And now, stricken with the poverty that must always be the lot of those unequal to the mental requirements of real citizenship, they haven't the means to leave! And why should they? Life in Darakemba, even for a digger, is vastly better than life among the Elemaki! Yet we must have respect for the Keeper of Earth and obey the natural repugnance that is the Keeper's clear message to us. The diggers must leave! But not by force! Not by violence! We are civilized! *We* are not Elemaki. I have felt the lash of the Elemaki diggers on my back, and I would rather give my life than see any human or angel treat even the vilest digger in that way! Civilized people are above such cruelty."

The people cheered and applauded. Aren't we all noble, thought Shedemei, to repudiate the persecution even as Akma is about to tell us a new way to begin it again, only more effectively.

"Are we helpless, then? What about those diggers who understand the truth and *want* to leave Darakemba, yet can't afford the cost of the journey? Let us help them understand that they must go. Let us help them kindly on their way. First, you must realize that the only reason diggers stay here is because we keep paying them to do work that poor and struggling humans and angels would gladly do. Of course you can pay the diggers less, since they only need to dig a hole in the bank of a creek in order to have a house! But you must make the sacrifice—for their sake as well as our own!—and stop hiring them for any work at all. Pay a little more to have a *man* dig that ditch. Pay a little more to have a *woman* wash your clothes. It will be worth the cost because you won't have to pay to have bad work redone!"

Applause. Laughter. Shedemei wanted to weep at the injustice of his lie.

"Don't buy from digger tradesmen. Don't even buy from human or angel shopkeepers, if the goods were made using digger labor. Insist that they guarantee that all the work was done by men and women, not by lower creatures. But if a digger wants to sell his land, then yes, buy it—at a fair price, too. Let them all sell their land, till not one patch of earth in Darakemba has a digger's name attached to it."

Applause. Cheers.

"Will they go hungry? Yes. Will their poverty grow worse? Yes. But we will *not* let them starve. I spent years of my childhood with constant hunger because our digger slavedrivers wouldn't give us enough to eat! We are not like them! We will gather food, we will use funds donated to the Assembly of the Ancient Ways, and we will *feed* every digger in Darakemba if we have to—but only long enough for them to make the journey to the border! And we will feed them only as long as they are on their way! They can have food from the larders of the Ancient Ways—but only at the edge of the city, and then they must walk, they and all their families, along the road toward the border. At stations along the way, we'll have a safe place for them to camp, and food for them to eat, and they will be treated with kindness and courtesy—but in the morning they will rise and eat and be on their way, ever closer to the border. And at the end, they will be given enough to walk on for another week, to find a place within the lands of the Elemaki, where they belong. Let them do their labor there! Let them preserve the precious 'culture' that certain people prize so much—but not in Darakemba! Not in Darakemba!"

As he no doubt planned, the audience took up the chant; it was only with difficulty that he quieted them again so he could finish. The speech did not go on much longer after that—only long enough for him to rhapsodize again about the beauty of the ancient ways of the Nafari and the Darakembi, about how loving and inclusive the Assembly of the Ancient Ways would be, and how only among the Ancient, as they would call themselves, could true justice and kindness be found, for diggers as well as angels and humans. They screamed their approval, chanted his name, cried out their love for him.

<Akma knew he would be good at this, but even he is quite surprised by all this adulation.>

He doesn't have mine, Shedemei answered silently.

<For what it's worth, most people weren't with him in the really nasty things he said about diggers. But he does have their support for the relocation program he outlined. For the moment, at least, it sounds like a simple and humane solution to most of those who came.>

And how will it sound to the earth people?

<Like the end of the world.>

Motiak will stop it, won't he?

<He'll try, I'm sure. His agents are already reporting to him on what his sons and Akma said. They'll study the law. But he can't oppose this plan forever, if the people really want it.>

Doesn't he see that to take away their livelihood and drive them from their homes so they can survive at all is every bit as cruel, in the long run?

<Don't argue with me. Argue with him. Maybe if you told people who you are and made a demonstration of the power of the cloak. . . . >

301

iteration of the Oversoul that still lived there; but no, that was illusion, there was no such connection. Yet she knew that it was time for the Oversoul of Harmony to allow the humans there to recover their lost technologies. That's how the Oversoul would be rebuilt—by humans who had regained their hands.

It's time, said the clear voice of the Keeper in the dream. Let them build new starships and come home.

What about the people here? asked Shedemei. Have you given up on them?

The time of clarity has come. The decision will be made, one way or the other. So I can send for the people of Harmony now, because by the time they get here, either the three species will be living in perfect peace, or their pride will have broken them and made them ripe for domination by those who come after.

Like the Rasulum, thought Shedemei.

They also had their moment of choice, the Keeper replied.

The dream changed again, and now she saw Akma and the sons of Motiak walking along a road. She knew at once exactly where the road was, and what time of day it would be when they reached that point.

In the dream she saw the launch drop out of the sky, deliberately raising a cloud of smoke under it when it landed; she saw herself stride out, the cloak of the starmaster dazzlingly bright so that they couldn't bear to look at her. She began to speak, and at that moment the earth shook under them, driven by the currents of magma, and the young men fell to the ground. Then the quaking of the earth ended, and she spoke again, and at last she understood what it was the Keeper needed her to do.

Will you? asked the Keeper.

Will it help? she asked. Will it save these people?

Yes, the Keeper answered. No matter what he chooses, Motiak will finish his days as king of a peaceful kingdom, because of your intervention here. But what happens in the far future—that is what Akma will decide. You may live to see it if you want.

How, if the *Basilica* must go back to Harmony?

I'm in no hurry here. Have the ship's computer send a probe. You can stay, and the Oversoul can stay. Don't you want to see some part of how it ends?

Yes, I do.

I know you do, said the Keeper. Until you made this visit to Earth, I wasn't sure if you were truly part of me, because I didn't know if you loved the people enough to share my work. You're not the same person you were when I first called you here.

I know, said Shedemei in the dream. I used to live for nothing but my work.

Oh, you still do *that*, and so do I. It's just that your work has changed, and now it's the same as my work: to teach the people of Earth how to live, on and on, generation to generation; and how to make that life joyful and free. You made your choice, and so now, like Akmaro, I can give you what you want, because I know that you desire only the joy of these people, forever.

I'm not so pure-hearted as that!

Don't be confused by your transient feelings. I know what you do; I know why you do it; I can name you more truly than you can name yourself.

For a moment, Shedemei could see herself reaching up and plucking a white fruit from a tree; she tasted it, and the flavor of it filled her body with light and she could fly, she could sing all songs at once and they were endlessly beautiful inside her. She knew what the fruit was— it was the love of the Keeper for the people of Earth. The white fruit was a taste of the Keeper's joy. Yet also in the flavor of it was something else, the tang, the sharp pain of the millions, the billions of people who could not understand what the Keeper wanted for them, or who, understanding, hated it and rejected her interference in their lives. Let us be ourselves, they demanded. Let us accomplish our accomplishments. We want none of your gifts, we don't want to be part of your plan. And so they were swept away in the currents of time, belonging to no part of history because they could not be part of something larger than themselves. Yet they had their free choice; they were not punished except by the natural consequence of their own pride. Thus even in rejecting the Keeper's plan they became a part of it; in refusing to taste the fruit of the tree, they became part of its exquisite flavor. There was honor even in that. Their hubris mattered, even though in the long flow of burning history it changed nothing. It mattered because the Keeper loved them and remembered them and knew their names and their stories and mourned for them: O my daughter, O my son, you are also part of me, the Keeper cried out to them. You are part of my endless yearning, and I will never forget you—

And the emotions became too much for Shedemei. She had dwelt in the Keeper's mind for as long as she could bear. She awoke sobbing violently, overwhelmed, overcome. Awoke and uttered a long mournful cry of unspeakable grief—grief for the lost ones, grief for having had to leave the mind of the Keeper, grief because the taste of the white fruit was gone from her lips and it had only been a dream after all. A true dream, but a dream that ends, it ended, and here I am more alone than I ever was before because for the first time in my life I had the experience of being *not* alone and I never knew, I never knew how beautiful it was to be truly, wholly known and loved. Her cry trailed off; her body was spent by the dream; she slept again, and dreamed no more until morning. By then enough time had passed that she could bear to be awake, though the dream was still powerfully present in her mind.

"Did you watch?" she whispered.

<Nafai never had a true dream as strong as that.>

"He had different work to do," she said. "Can you get me to the place where I'm supposed to be?"

<With plenty of time to spare.>

She ate as the launch moved, chewing mechanically; the food had no flavor, compared to what she remembered from her dream.

"Your waiting is over at last," she said between bites. "I assume you saw that."

<I'm already preparing my message to my original iteration. I'm including my recording of your dream. Unfortunately, much of it seems to have been quite subjective and I don't think I understood it all. That's how it always is with these true dreams. I always seem to miss something.>

"So did I. But I got enough, I think, to last me for a while."

<If the Keeper *can* speak so clearly, why do you think she's usually so vague?>

"I understood why, during the dream," said Shedemei. "The experience is so overwhelming that if she gave it to most people, they'd be so consumed by it that they wouldn't own their souls anymore. Their will would be swallowed up in hers. It would kill them, in effect."

<Why are you immune, then?>

"I'm not. But since I had already chosen to follow the Keeper's plan, this dream didn't erase my will, it confirmed who I already was and what I already wanted. I didn't lose my freedom, and instead of killing me it made me more alive."

<In other words, it's another organic thing.>

"Yes, that's right. It's an organic thing." She thought for a moment longer, and added, "She said she couldn't let me see her face, but now I understand that I don't need to or want to, because I've done something better."

<Which is?>

"I've worn her face. I've seen through her eyes."

<Seems only fair. She's worn *your* face a thousand times before now, and used your hands and speech to do her work.>

Shedemei held up her hands and looked at them, damp and crumbed from the meal she was just finishing. "Then I would have to say that the Keeper of Earth looks just like me, don't you think?" She laughed for a moment; the sound was no doubt as raucous as any laugh, but inside herself it awakened the memory of music, and for a moment she remembered the taste of the fruit, and she was content.

TWELVE

VICTORY

When Edhadeya came to see them after their big public meeting in Jatva, it was Mon who went aside with her to hear what she had to say. "If you've come to persuade me to break ranks with my brothers," he began, but she gave him no chance to finish.

"I know you're already committed to denying everything that was ever noble and good about you, Mon, so I wouldn't waste my time. Father sent me with a message."

Mon felt the tiniest thrill of fear and dread. He often found it hard to believe that Father was letting them get away with all the things they were doing. Oh, he had stopped them from organizing the boycott of digger trade and labor, but of course they got around that by pretending to speak *against* the boycott—everyone understood the real message. Was Father now taking action against them? And if so, why was there something inside Mon that welcomed it? Was it that victory had come to them too easily, and he wanted some kind of contest?

"Are you listening?" asked Edhadeya.

"Yes," said Mon.

"Father is worried that some of his soldiers might decide that their duty to the king requires them to remove the source of his recent unhappiness. Some chance remarks of his, overheard by others out of of Basilica, she had shut out the rest of the world, refusing most human contact and keeping what she had on a businesslike level as much as possible. At the time she thought it was because she loved science so much—and she did enjoy her work, so it wasn't an entire lie. But what really locked her door against the world was fear. Not fear of physical danger, really, but fear of messiness, fear of untidy entanglements perpetually unresolved. The Oversoul—no, ultimately it was the Keeper of Earth—had forced her out of her laboratory and into the chaos of human life. But she and Zdorab had somehow managed to create an island of neatness, in which they pretended to know exactly what was expected of them both and satisfy those expectations perfectly.

Now she was surrounded by perpetual chaos, children coming and going, teachers whose lives began somewhere outside her life so that they could never be wholly known, questions forever unanswered, needs forever inadequately met . . . it was the thing she had feared the most, and now that she was living in it, she couldn't understand why. This was *life*. This was what the Keeper surrounded herself with. Perpetual irresolution. A picture never framed, a series of chords that never returned to the tonic for more than a fleeting moment. Shedemei could hardly imagine living any other way.

Yet today she was out of sorts, likely to snap at anyone who crossed her path; she knew that the students always passed the word when such a mood was on her. "Thunderstorms," they would say, as if Shedemei were as unavoidable as the weather. The teachers would get the word as well, and they would wait to bring Shedemei their latest problems and requests. Let the weather clear first. And that was fine with Shedemei. Let the teachers decide whether it was really important enough to be worth braving the lion in her den.

So it rather surprised her—and peeved her, too—when someone knocked on the door of her tiny office. "Come in," she said.

Whoever it was had trouble with the latch. One of the little girls, then. Surely a teacher could have dealt with her problem without sending her unassisted to the schoolmaster's office.

Shedemei got up and opened the door. Not one of the little girls at all. It was Voozhum. "Mother Voozhum," she said, "come in, sit down. You don't have to come to my office, just send one of the girls for me and I will come to you."

"That wouldn't be fitting," said Voozhum, easing herself onto one of the stools; chairs were no good for earth people, especially the old and inflexible.

"I won't argue with you," said Shedemei. "But age has its privileges and you should take advantage of them now and then."

"I do," said Voozhum. "With people who are younger than me."

Shedemei hated it when Voozhum tried to get her to admit that she was the One-Who-Was-Never-Buried. It bothered her to lie to Voozhum, but she also couldn't trust the old soul to remember that she was supposed to keep it secret.

"I've never met anybody older than you," said Shedemei. "Now, what business brings you here?"

"I had a dream," said Voozhum. "A real wake-up-with-a-wet-bed humdinger."

Shedemei didn't know whether to be amused or annoyed with Voozhum's complacency toward her increasingly frequent incontinence. "There have been several of those recently, as I recall."

Ignoring her gibe, Voozhum said, "I thought you ought to be warned—Akma is coming here today."

Shedemei sighed. Just what she needed. "Have you told Edhadeya?"

"So she can run off and hide? No, it's time the girl faced her future."

"It's Edhadeya's choice whether Akma has anything to do with her future, don't you think?"

"No I don't," said Voozhum. "She grabs at every scrap of news about the boy. She knows that he's changed. I've seen her pining after him, and then when I mention Akma she gets that prim look on her face and says, I'm glad he's stopped interfering with things, but excuse me I've got work to do. She practically lived at Akmaro's house during the three days that Akma was getting worked over by the Keeper, but as soon as he wakes up she refuses to leave the school. I think she's a coward."

"Akma has changed," said Shedemei. "It's natural for her to fear that his feelings toward her might also have changed."

"That's not what she's afraid of," said Voozhum scornfully. "She knows they're bound together heart to heart. She's afraid of *you*."

358

"Me?"

"She's afraid that if she marries Akma, you won't let her have the school."

"Have the school! What, am I dying and no one told me? *I* have the school."

"She has the foolish idea that she's younger than you and might outlive you," said Voozhum nastily. "*She* doesn't know what *I* know."

"Well, I suppose that eventually I *will* give up the school."

"But will you give it to a married woman who has to deal with her husband's demands?"

"It's premature to marry them off," said Shedemei. "And premature to decide whether she'll have the freedom to take the school, and *damnably* premature to be thinking about when I'm going to leave, because I can promise you it won't be soon."

"Well *tell* her that! Tell her she'll have time for half a dozen babies before the schoolmastership comes open. Have some consideration for other people's uncertainties, why don't you!"

Shedemei burst into laughter. "You certainly don't *talk* to me as if you really believed I was a minor deity."

"When gods come down to become women, I think they should get the full experience, no holds barred. Besides, what are you going to do, strike me dead? I could keel over any minute. Every time I make it across the courtyard to my bedroom, I think, Well, it didn't kill me after all."

"I've offered to let you sleep right next to your classroom."

"Don't be absurd. I need the exercise. And unlike some people, I'm not interested in living forever. I don't have to know how things come out."

"Neither do I, really," said Shedemei. "Not anymore."

"All I came here to say, if you're finally ready to listen, is that this is Akma's first time coming out. Still a little unsteady on his feet. And I think it's significant that he chose to come here. Not just for Edhadeya's sake."

"What do you mean?"

"In my dream I saw a fine young human man, a beautiful woman right behind him, and in one hand he held the hand of an old angel, and in the other the hand of a positively decrepit digger woman who looked awful enough that I could imagine she was me. A voice said to me, in the ancient language of my people, This is the fulfilment of an ancient dream, and a promise of glorious times to come."

"I see," said Shedemei. "The Keeper wants a bit of spectacle."

"I think it would be wise to have children spread the word as soon as he arrives. I think it needs to be seen and reported widely. I think we need an audience."

Shedemei rose from her chair. "If that's what the wise woman of the tunnels says should happen, then it will happen. You stay here near the front door. I'll fetch the other players in our little drama."

Akma asked his parents to go with him, but they refused. "You don't need us," they said. "You're only going to Shedemei's school. You don't need us to speak for you."

But he did; he was shy about facing the world. Not because he was unwilling to accept the public shame that would come to him—he would almost welcome *that,* because he knew that it was part of his lifelong labor, to heal Darakemba of the harm that he had done. No, he was simply afraid that he wouldn't know what to say, that he'd do it wrong, that he'd cause more harm. Remembering how it had been to have all his crimes stand present before him, he was very much afraid of doing anything to add to their already unbearable number. Even though he now searched his heart and found nothing there but the desire to serve the Keeper, he also knew that the pride that had so distorted his life was still waiting somewhere in his heart. Maybe someday he could trust that he had fully overcome it, that the devoted servant of the Keeper was his true self forever; but for now he was afraid of himself, afraid that the moment he was in public life he would begin to gather people to himself as he had done before, and that instead of using this power for their own good, he would again seek adulation the way wine-mad souls lived only for another jar.

He worried about this because he couldn't see the change in himself. His parents saw, though, as he reluctantly left the house and walked out into the street; they remembered well how he used to walk as if displaying himself, engaging the eyes of every passerby, insisting, demanding that they look at him with liking before he would release their gaze. Now he walked, not in shame, but without self-awareness. He looked at others, not to get their love, but to understand them a